Enemies destroy the lake people's village and cap-
ture Arvi's father, the chief. Arvi finds a way to build
a shelter on his father's fishing raft on the lake. How
his idea grows into a whole village of lake dwellings
and how his people finally defeat their enemies makes
an interesting and exciting story.

THE FIRST LAKE DWELLERS

BY CHESTER G. OSBORNE

With a foreword by Melville J. Herskovits
Department of Anthropology, Northwestern University

ILLUSTRATIONS BY RICHARD N. OSBORNE

Follett Publishing Company

CHICAGO

LIBRARY OF CONGRESS CATALOG CARD NUMBER: 56-5121

Preface

This book takes us still another step along the track man has traced in his endeavor to attain security by mastering his environment and protecting himself against his enemies, animal and human. In *The First Bow and Arrow,* Mr. Osborne has told how the inventiveness of human beings brought them to adapt a physical device to aid them in survival. In *The First Puppy* we see this same creativeness in man bringing some of the animals in his environment under his control, and thus further extending his power over the natural forces with which he had to contend. Here, Mr. Osborne deals with the discovery by man of certain forces latent in himself, telling us how the tradition of mutual aid that has always marked the life of human groups was harnessed to create settled community living.

The social setting is here far more complicated than in the earlier books. We find organized human groups warring with each other; we learn of traders who traverse great distances taking the products of one people to another. More, we see how Shomu, the wise old man, realized the need to preserve the seed for sowing, however great the hunger of the people, so that the next year could provide its crop. We are far from the simple horde of the Old Stone Age, depending on the chance good fortune of the hunt, or on finding a tree bearing nuts or berries.

V. Gordon Childe, the British archaeologist, has described three economic revolutions during man's history. The first came when man established settled agricultural communities; the second when the city developed, in the basin of the Eastern Mediterranean; the third when the power machine was discovered and brought on the Industrial Era. Today, when we stand at the threshold of an Atomic Age, it is good for us all, young or old, to understand the continuities of human experience, by turning back to the time when the first great change in man's way of life took place.

It is of this fascinating period, the Neolithic Revolution, when man established his modes of settled community living, that Mr. Osborne writes so engagingly in this book. Reading it cannot but help the reader to attain the historical perspective that was never more needed than today.

MELVILLE J. HERSKOVITS

Department of Anthropology

Northwestern University

THE FIRST
LAKE DWELLERS

Warning from the Forest

A SHRILL, eerie whistle sounded and echoed in the woods. Then there was a distant call.

Arvi paused in his work of tying grain into sheaves and looked warily across the stubbly fields. No wild animal or bird moved. No wind rustled in the trees.

But Arvi frowned and backed away. The sounds were strange; until he could identify them, it would be safer to

move from the edge of the wilderness—the vast northern forest around the clearing, the village, and the lake.

Down the lower slope of the field his mother and sister hurried towards the village. They had cut most of the barley and millet and now were carrying away some of the sheaves he had bound earlier. On the lake, dugout canoes were as small as toys in the haze of morning. On his great

raft at the shore, Arvi's father stored a fishing net in the raft hut. Nearby, a party of hunters marched out through the palisade that surrounded the long thatched houses.

The whistle cut through the forest again, louder and nearer. Arvi whirled around, his dark eyes wide in alarm. He was but twelve years old; all he had for a weapon was his flint knife. He must flee. He sped across the field and threw himself down behind a pile of stumps. An arrow dug into a branch near his head, and he shouted to his father, "Hawk! Calling Hawk!"

A bowstring twanged. Another arrow flew, its point a shining blur in the sun. It clattered into the stumps. A twig crackled. Arvi hurled his knife at the sound, then bounded away like a frightened deer.

No other sounds followed. At the foot of the field Calling Hawk ran to him and thrust a harpoon into his hands; he had another in his own. "Someone shot at me," Arvi panted. "The arrows came so close I could see the points shine!"

"I heard strange sounds—" Hawk's deep-set eyes were intent on the forest.

8

"I threw my knife, hoping I would make someone step aside for long enough to give me a start."

"You did the right thing." Hawk's lean, rugged face showed his worry. "There could be the worst kind of danger. Trotting Fox is near, leaving on a hunt, and may have heard that whistling too. We'll ask him."

They hurried down the path. Rounding a turn by the

lake, they saw the hunters Arvi had seen from the hillside. Most of the men were bearded, and all were armed with bows, spears, and javelins.

Trotting Fox signaled a halt. He was tall, and his eyes were small as those of a fox; around his neck he wore a string of fox paws.

"There are enemies in the forest," Calling Hawk said quickly. "Someone shot at Arvi."

"Who made that whistling sound?" asked Woran the hunter.

"We do not know." Hawk watched Trotting Fox closely. "The lad says that the arrows gleamed as they flew."

A murmur arose from the hunters. "The Shining Stones!"

Trotting Fox glanced up towards the clearing where Hawk, Ruru, and a few others raised their crops of wheat, barley, and millet. "The boy imagines things." He squinted at Arvi. "Harvesting is the work of women. Why were you in the field?"

Cub Fox, a bristly-haired youth who was the young-est brother of the hunting chieftain, grinned broadly. Arvi

10

flushed as the men stared at him. "I was tying the grain. We must get it into the storage pits and granary while the weather is still dry."

"Arvi follows my orders," Hawk said curtly.

"He could hunt with us," Trotting Fox said.

Hawk scowled. "The grain comes first. I am chieftain of the village in civil affairs and in matters like these; raising grain is my problem.

"But you are leader in times of battle. Rather than talking here, you should be hurrying to the field to see if there is danger. You are armed. We have only harpoons."

"Show us the place," Trotting Fox said. "I would see the shiny arrows." He motioned to Arvi to lead the way.

The youth walked toward the heap of stumps. "The arrows fell here."

"Everyone will look." Trotting Fox thrust his spear at the rough ground, pushing stalks and twigs aside. His men circled about, eyes on the soil.

Hawk searched, too, but several times he stared up at the trees. "We are easy targets," he warned. "We stand in the open—"

11

"Tend to your farming," Trotting Fox interrupted. "I am leader in this."

Snapping Fish called out, "I see nothing."

"There are no arrows over here," Grebe reported.

Trotting Fox poked impatiently at the stumps. "If the field is dangerous, Hawk, it might be wise for you and the boy to stay close to the village. But I can delay no longer. I have far to go." He beckoned to his men, and with them hastened away into the forest.

Hawk took Arvi by the arm. "We'll take the bundles that are ready and go back. Nearly all the harvest is in."

Quickly they picked up the sheaves and started back to the village. "You held your temper well for a youth," Hawk said.

"I wish I were going with them," Arvi declared.

"You and I will hunt after we have stored the seed and milled the grain, and after the flax is prepared. The Fox brothers have no respect for this, but grain is where we put it; we do not have to chase it over hill and mountain only perhaps to lose it in the end."

Arvi glanced back as if he once again expected to hear

12

the eerie whistle. "That sound still rings in my ears. And the arrows—I really saw them. Could someone have taken them while we were talking to Trotting Fox?"

"Yes," Hawk said grimly. "And they may still be near. When we get home, Lani and Londa can finish with the grain. I will see Shomu and ask his advice. Then you and I will look to our weapons. We may need them!"

The village was a cluster of long huts on the lake shore. It was encircled by a high fence of sharpened stakes. The gate was open; Hawk frowned when he saw it so, and slammed it shut. For a moment he scanned the palisade, estimating its strength and the position of the lookout mounds which stood behind it. Frowning deeper, he looked across the village clearing at the people who were curing hides and smoking fish. Then he turned to his own dwelling.

He and Arvi pushed past the goats which were tied at the entrance and went in to stack the sheaves in a corner.

Lani, Arvi's mother, greeted them. "We have separated much of the seed; some is in the pits in the floor and the rest in the granary." And, seeing the troubled expression on Hawk's face, she went on, "What has happened?"

"There are strangers in the forest." Hawk told of the incident. "They may be the Shining Stones!"

"Who are they?" asked Arvi's sister, Londa. She was older than he, but because the youth was tall and of wiry build, they looked nearly the same age. Londa wore her hair in braids; like Lani, she was dressed in a scarlet skirt and a sleeveless jacket of rough linen squares sewn together.

"You may not remember, for they have not come into the mountain lands for several years. They are robbers. Their weapons are tipped with shiny polished stones; that is how they get their strange name.

"Our village is sometimes a mark for such groups of warlike people. We have the palisade, so that when the raiders are few, we can defend ourselves. But the Shining Stones are a horde. They are strong and fierce, and they are led by a chieftain who is greatly feared. Many tribes pay him a tribute to keep themselves safe."

"Warth!" Lani shuddered. "If he is near, we are in grave peril!"

"Why did our hunters go out this day?" Londa asked.

"They may return tonight," Arvi said.

14

Hawk paced the floor. "If there were men enough now, we could have a council. The next best thing to do is to speak to the One of Wisdom and Magic."

With a jar of wheat as a gift for Shomu, Arvi and Hawk went to the lonely hut where the older man lived. Near the door the chief called, "It is I, Hawk. I would speak with the One of Wisdom."

A quavery voice told them to enter the dark room.

"Arvi, my son, is with me to hear and remember," Hawk explained. Shomu did not reply at first. Village sounds seemed far away. So thick was the smoke that Arvi wanted to cough, but he dared not move. The eyes of the old man were sharp upon him.

"Trouble has brought you to me," Shomu said finally.

"The Shining Stones." Hawk told the story.

Shomu's voice trembled. "The whistle may have been a voice of a Night Spirit. Did it sound like an owl?"

Hawk nodded for the boy to reply. "It was too thin a sound—it cut like a knife! Besides, there were the arrows."

"This is bad news." Shomu rocked back and forth. "Trotting Fox should have stayed. Once before, Warth chose this very month for a raid: the crops are in; the sturgeon and pickerel have been caught; the women have made baskets of reeds and utensils of clay and wood. It would be the time for the Shining Stones to capture many prizes. But surely Trotting Fox knows—"

"He knows," Hawk pointed out, "but he places small value on the grains, and would have us all live like hunters. Further, he did not believe Arvi's story."

"I believe the youth." Shomu nodded in approval. "From your account, Hawk, he did well to hold his temper when Cub and the others spoke as they did. That is a mark of a leader. But—something else troubles you, Hawk!"

"The palisade." Hawk drew a deep breath. "If Warth hits us in full strength, the palisade will not hold!"

The Magic of the Fire

THE OLD MAN sat still. "Not hold! If you say that, Hawk, I believe it, too, for you are a chief—"

"Only in civil matters," Hawk reminded him. "I do not want the duties of Trotting Fox."

"You could take over his leadership. You are as quick on the hunt and as strong in warfare."

When Hawk shook his head, Shomu persisted. "Times change. We have always had one leader for battle, another for the village, and one like Snapping Fish for managing the fishing. But your way with farming has changed everything. You have encouraged the families of Ruru and Bending Branch to clear the fields, to plant, to catch the wild goats and tame them. Now we can eat well all year round instead of feasting in the summer and starving in the winter as we once did.

"Food is saved for the winter. It must be defended. We are wandering hunters no more. Our lives change, and our plan of leadership must also: there should be one chief. If the council meets, I, Shomu, will tell them."

Hawk exclaimed, "But Trotting Fox—"

"He can be your lieutenant. He is needed as before, but must accept you as the final leader."

Hawk thought it over. "If it were the wish of the council—"

"The council will hear me, for I will ask help of the Spirits." He motioned to Hawk. "Now I would speak to the boy alone."

The village chieftain presented the gift of wheat, and went outside. There he saw that fear had fallen over the place; people whispered, pointed at the forest, and seemed to expect the Shining Stones to come any moment.

In the hut, Shomu spoke earnestly to the youth: "If Warth breaks in, he will steal or burn everything. Do you know what that means?"

"We should be hungry all winter," answered Arvi.

"Worse than that," Shomu quavered. "If he takes the

18

grain, he takes the seed for next spring also. Seed cannot be easily replaced. You must think of it as sacred. Without it, it would be years before we could plant again, and before then our people could perish. We cannot conceal the grain —it is too bulky. But one person could carry away and hide enough seed to start a small crop next year. A man might be noticed. But children often leave the village with jars to gather berries or to bring water from the lake. You could take some seed in jars into the forest and hide it.

"Hawk fears that the palisade might not hold back the enemy. If there is danger, then you must get away and flee with the seed to a place of safety. There hide the seed where it will remain dry against the weather, and tell no one what you have done."

Shomu watched Arvi carefully. "You must understand that Hawk cannot go. As a chieftain he must stay until the last. And if I told this plan to anyone else, then word would get out that I fear a defeat, and panic would sweep the village!"

Arvi said, "There will be some who would call me a coward if they see me run away and if I cannot explain.

When I return I should like it to be known that you sent me."

Shomu shook his head. "Even when the enemy goes away, there will be another danger. In the winter the people will be hungry. They will want food. There would be some who would want to take the seed and eat it then and there."

"They would not do such a thing!" Arvi said fearfully.

"They would." Shomu's eyes narrowed. "They would, for I have seen things like that happen. Some there are who cannot think ahead and plan for another day."

While Arvi stared in astonishment, the old man went on, "It will be best if you do just as I say *and never mention the seed to anyone, until it is time for planting again.*

"If the worst happens, you may thus save the village from further misery. If nothing happens, then you can laugh about it with the others."

"Some would laugh," Arvi said bitterly. "They have no respect for the work that Hawk and Ruru do." He looked at Shomu. "Where could I hide the seed—if I did escape?"

Then Shomu told of the Cave of the Ancient Ones.

20

Arvi knew it well. But Shomu told of a brooklet in the cave: when the water was low in late summer, one could wade along the brook into a tunnel and thence into a chamber in the depths. "It is a place few have seen," Shomu said. "Touch nothing that is there, lest you stir the wrath of the Spirits of the Ancient Ones who once dwelt there."

Soon after, Arvi rejoined his father; his face was pale. "Shomu talked much of the danger. He has given me a task to perform—but I am to keep it secret."

"Obey him," Hawk said briefly. "Now we have much to do in preparing our weapons."

Arvi said no more of his task, though Londa and Lani were curious when they saw him take several sacks of wheat, millet, and other grains and stuff them into two large jars. A jar under each arm, he hurried outside. "Another gift for Shomu?" Londa suggested.

But Arvi would not say, and Hawk shook his head warningly. "Shomu gave us some advice," he explained. "Some of it we may not discuss.

"But the rest is for anyone to know; I told him that the palisade might not hold under a siege."

"You told everyone that when the defenses were being built," Lani said. "I remember that you wanted a ditch around the village, and sharp stakes pointing out from the foot of the fence. Now everyone is worried and wishes that your advice had been followed. I think one chief would be the answer to our troubles."

"That is the answer Shomu offered," said Hawk. "But the people will have to work together, one leader or not. None wanted the kind of fence I suggested because of the work; they would have had to give up time and labor!"

"They'll give up more than that," Lani said, "if the Shining Stones get through!"

Hawk picked up a knife. "Arvi and I will make arrows. You and Londa should bring water from the lake. Use every jar and waterskin you can; there are more in the hut on our raft. We shall need them if there is a siege or a fire."

"A fire!" Londa was frightened.

"I wish the hunters would return," said Arvi as Lani and Londa hastened away. He sat down to help Hawk.

At dusk the hunters came, singing in triumph because

22

they had slain a wild boar and two elk. A noisy welcome
awaited them, not only because of their success, but also
because many of the villagers feared an attack.

Trotting Fox and Foxhead did not want a council;
they called for a feast and a dance; but the others had their
way. "We have no proof that Warth's men are near," Trotting Fox insisted. "If we had, I should not have taken the
hunters away."

"Several people heard the whistling," the carpenter,
Bending Branch, reminded him. "And you were one."

"This is the time Warth would choose," Ruru said.
"Our grain is harvested now."

"Grain!" Trotting Fox grunted. "Every year more of us depend on farming. That ties us down so that we must live and work near the fields. If all of us were hunters, we could pick up our belongings and go away if there was danger. Now we must stay and perhaps fight to defend the granary."

Calling Hawk said, "The grain defends us against starvation. Hunting gives us meat when we are successful, but it is not a certain thing."

"What of the enemy?" Grebe asked. "If the Shining Stones come, will the palisade hold? Hawk and some others wanted it stronger at one time."

"It will hold," Trotting Fox assured him. "We have lookout mounds from which we can shoot down at the enemy; he could not get close enough to destroy it."

"Who stands at the mounds now?" Hawk asked quietly.

The question startled everyone. Trotting Fox's face turned an angry red above his beard. "No one!" he retorted. "There is no danger!"

Foxhead spoke up. "The boys could be lookouts for now." He called to Cub Fox, "Get Arvi—"

24

"Not Arvi," Trotting Fox snapped. "He would see an evil spirit in every shadow."

"The others, then," Foxhead said. As Cub Fox hurried away, Shomu walked slowly towards the circle; there was a sudden hush.

"Speak to the council," Hawk said to Shomu. "Give us the Magic of the Fire. Watch the smoke, and tell us what you see!"

Shomu pulled his robe high over his shoulders. From his medicine bag he took a handful of powder and threw it at the flames. The men watched tensely.

The flames turned color. Smoke swirled up in dark clouds. "The smoke rises in several ways, with the many winds," Shomu muttered. "So is the village divided.

"One smoke goes to the trees. There the Spirits of the Night Birds warn us. One smoke goes to the marshes and to the south. The Evil Spirits are there. One smoke goes over the lake. The Evil Spirits cannot reach across the water. One smoke goes low over the village. It is a bad sign."

"What does that mean?" someone asked. But the One of Wisdom shook his head. "No more of the prophecy can I explain." The men talked excitedly. Trotting Fox said, "The men fear an attack. What should we do?"

"The village is different from what it was in olden times," Shomu said. And he spoke long, telling the council much of what he had told Hawk and Arvi earlier.

Standing in the doorway of his dwelling, Arvi heard most of the talk, for it was not secret. Enviously he watched Cub Fox, Ousel, and several other older boys standing at

the lookout places with bows and arrows. But he was more concerned with what the men would decide.

"One chieftain!" he heard Trotting Fox exclaim. "Who would lead on the hunt if Calling Hawk were chief?"

"You would," Shomu replied, "but under Hawk's orders."

The battle chief hesitated. "I would not object as much as some might think," he finally said. "I would still be on the council. And the responsibility I have is a heavy one. See how it has been today: no matter what we decide, there will be argument. A chief is someone to blame when things go wrong!

"A single chief might be better, but is Hawk the one?"

"I favor Calling Hawk," Shomu began, but a roar of argument drowned his words.

"They had better decide on someone," Arvi said to Lani. But when Calling Hawk came home a long time after, no decision had been agreed upon save one: guards would be posted.

"What of the prophecy?" the boy asked. "I do not understand it."

"Nor do I. Shomu is a One of Magic and can call the spirits and see visions in the ritual of fire. But he lets the messages speak for themselves. I understood but one phrase, that the village is divided. He meant that we have too many selfish people, and too few who will work together."

It was late when Arvi awoke. The eerie whistle seemed to ring again in his ears. Quickly he slipped into his clothes and ran past the goats as they tugged at their ropes. Dogs barked noisily. A guard shouted, "Someone moves in the forest!"

Calling Hawk was beside him then. A burning arrow flashed like lightning across the dark sky. "The Shining Stones!" someone yelled. The men ran from their huts. Another arrow and still another flew across the clearing.

"Stand on the mounds!" Trotting Fox shouted. "They have a fire to light their arrows. We can see to shoot—"

"If they get into the trees, they will see us, too," Hawk muttered. "That campfire should be out." He and Arvi kicked dirt over the embers. Beyond the palisade the battle cries of the enemy came louder, and the villagers rushed to defend themselves. Hawk pointed out a lookout place at the west side for Arvi and then raced to join the others.

With the fire dimmed, the village was dark for a moment. Then a thatched roof burst into flames. From his high place Arvi peered cautiously over the palisade. Just beyond bowshot were scores of warriors spreading out from the forest trail. Some carried torches, so that the night was

filled with flickering lights and skulking shadows. Others moved to encircle the village.

An arrow smashed against the fence. Arvi ducked. The strange cries of the enemy were mixed with the defiant yells of the villagers, and Trotting Fox's voice rose: "They carry a battering ram to the gate. Shoot them down!"

"There are others on the lake side!" Snapping Fish yelled.

Arvi took aim with an arrow: then the palisade quivered under his hand. There was a crash at the gate. In the glow of burning houses he saw the dark shapes of Trotting Fox and several others as they hurled their spears: beneath them the enemy battered at the gate.

"It will not hold!" He heard Calling Hawk's voice.

Arvi crouched behind the shaky fence. Shomu's orders came to his mind, and he remembered Hawk's curt response: "Obey him." He dropped his bow, reached up, and with trembling hands took hold of the top of the palisade. His fingers closed on the rough wooden points. For an instant he held on, then turned sideways and flung himself over.

30

Escape in the Night

THE SHOCK of landing threw Arvi to his knees. He backed against the fence. Which way would be safest?

The palisade shook violently as the log crashed into the gate. The Shining Stones roared in fury.

Arvi darted into the forest. A few paces on, he groped in a bush for the clay jars. They were safe!

Someone shouted harshly; a branch snapped; shadows rose up. "They have seen me!" he whispered. He snatched up the jars and ran towards the marshes. Behind him the sky brightened with fire. There was another yell, closer.

As the boy gained the marshland, the long grass twisted at his ankles. But the trail he wanted was this way; it led to the shore and to a canoe on the bank of Black River. His speed slowed as his feet sank into the mud; the jars seemed heavier and clumsier.

The ground hardened suddenly. This was the trail. He followed it from memory, running headlong into the gloom.

A dark shape arose. A long arm reached out. Arvi yelled in fright and leaped off the trail. The shadow followed. He floundered about, holding the jars high, and stumbled back towards the path. There was a splashing behind him.

On he raced, to the open starlight of the beach. If he could reach a dugout that was moored near the inlet, he might escape. It should be just a few paces ahead—but footsteps grated nearby. Then his feet splashed into the black water of the inlet. There was the canoe. He tugged at the heavy prow.

He heard quick steps. The canoe was torn from his grasp. Arvi grabbed one of the paddles, but the stranger spoke in his own language. "You need not fight—" The boy saw the canoe slide into the water as if pushed by a giant. "Climb in—quickly—"

Arvi held the paddle ready. "Who are you?"

The shadowy form tossed a spear and javelin into the

dugout, then snatched the paddle from Arvi. The voice was deep: "Get in, or I'll leave you. Others saw you leave the village."

Arvi saw torches blaze on the swamp trail.

"Those are Warth's men. They seek both you and me. Now come with me or else stay here alone."

There was no other escape. Arvi seized the jars and put them in the dugout. It lurched away almost as he got in.

An arrow brushed his shoulder. The stranger shoved the paddle hard against the bank and knelt down as the craft swung into the current. "Which way? Quickly!"

Arvi twisted up to see the stars. "South." The dugout leaped forward. Along the shore shouts echoed. Cautiously, Arvi lifted his head. "Two men are coming right out after us," he cried.

"Take this." The stranger thrust the paddle into Arvi's hands and crouched forward. The head of his spear glistened. There was a cry and a thrashing.

Arvi had taken two strokes with the paddle when he felt the blade almost yanked from his grasp. He wrenched it free and in desperation swung it down. It hit. Arvi gripped the paddle anew and forced the craft out into deep water. "Faster!" the stranger urged.

Arvi put all his strength into each stroke. The stranger waited, javelin ready. "Get us out of bowshot!"

Another arrow plummeted into the water. "That one fell behind us," the voice said. "They can't reach us now. Get your breath. Then go on. You handle the craft well. And you must know a safe place. I'll keep watch."

Breathing hard, Arvi looked back. Torches lit the shore, but his companion's face was still obscure. The boy hesitated. His mission should be a secret: but the stranger seemed to intend no harm and had already proved a powerful ally. "Go on," the man warned.

"I don't know what else I can do," Arvi said. He slid the blade into the water. The stranger chuckled and sat back more comfortably. Silently they glided around a point of land. The torches were blotted out; the darkness grew thicker. At last Arvi swung west; the dugout grated on sand.

"Ashore here," he whispered. The stranger slid over the side to hold the prow. Balancing the jars carefully, Arvi

34

stepped into the shallows and listened. An owl hooted; the low waves splashed softly.

"We can hide the canoe. The underbrush grows thick here." The stranger heaved the canoe onto the bank. They slid it into the bushes and pulled the branches together behind it. The stranger seemed content to follow the boy's directions.

"Onto the ledge." Arvi picked up the jars and in the dull moonlight hastened up a slope. Once he glanced back and saw the stranger's face, painted thickly with ugly stripes. But a long hand pointed ahead.

They climbed another ledge and a path like a goat trail that twisted up a cliff. The boy stopped soon. "There is a cave near here. Sometimes one can hear the rush of the brook that runs through it."

They listened. Arvi said "Left," and they plodded on until the trail seemed to stop. Arvi slid into a crevice. "This is the Cave of the Ancient Ones," he said, and an echo came back, "Ancient Ones." Wearily he set the jars down. They looked back anxiously.

The moon lit a broad path across the lake. Arvi started; far to the north the sky was red.

"The whole village is afire!" Arvi's voice trembled. "What will become of my people? I should go back—the Shining Stones may be winning—"

"Stay here!" A strong hand gripped his shoulder. "You could not help."

The tall form blocked the narrow entrance completely. Arvi asked, "Who are you?"

"I am Quara." The deep voice was softer. "Lie down, Fleet One, and try to rest."

Arvi slumped against the cold wall of the cave. His arms and legs ached; his clothing was wet with mud. For a few moments he lay tense, listening. But he heard only the chirp of a cricket and the bubbling of the stream somewhere in the back of the cavern. He fell asleep.

Help from a Stranger

BRIGHT SUNLIGHT awoke him. When he saw where he was, he stood up in alarm. But the jars were safe.

Quara's lanky figure lay blocking the entrance; he was even taller than the boy had thought. The tanned, bony face was clean shaven and streaked with red and white paint. A leather helmet partly covered his yellow hair and was tipped over his eyes; a loose tunic was bound at the waist with a wide belt; the long legs were clad in elkskin trousers laced to his knees.

Arvi sought the stranger's weapons. The short javelin was beyond his reach. But in one outstretched hand was a knife of green stone; the lean fingers were draped loosely over the staghorn handle.

Cautiously the boy reached out. Quara grunted. Arvi jumped back. After a moment he reached down again.

He had it. Confused and shaking, he stepped back. When he looked up, the stranger had pushed up the leather helmet and was watching him.

Sharp blue eyes twinkled. "Now that you have my knife, what are you going to do with it?"

The boy tossed the knife to the ground. "I do not think that you intend to harm me, for you could have done so before now. And I remember that you slew one of the Shining Stones so that I could escape."

"So that *we* could escape," the man corrected him. He

sat up, scratching at his long yellow hair and yawning. "You slew one yourself: a mighty blow it was, too."

He chuckled. "And what a chase you led me! I do not know your name, but I would call you the Fleet One." Arvi smiled wryly as Quara went on, "I was a prisoner, too, even more than you have been, because soon you will be free. I held you here because the forest was no place for a lad with all those savages storming about."

He looked out through the narrow crevice. "I am going to get my packs. If the way is clear, I shall come back and tell you. Wait here."

The stranger hurried down the cliff as nimbly as a long-legged spider. The leather helmet bobbed into the trees below and vanished. The lake was quiet, but over the northern shore smoke rose in gray lines. Where Black River met the lake, a crane on one leg waited like a lonely fisherman. A grebe dove into the water. The birds showed no fear, and Arvi knew that no man moved nearby.

He drew back, worry and fear seizing him. What had happened? Was his family safe? Then his eyes fell on the jars: they must be hidden.

The brooklet was low, as the One of Wisdom had said; it vanished into a dark place. He would need a torch.

Arvi found a branch of pitchy pine; with dry moss and flints from a pouch at his belt, he set it blazing. Then he carried the jars one at a time to the tunnel and to the room beyond; it was a vast place. He put the jars high on a rocky ledge, and as he went out the last time, he held the torch high. Pictures of bears and of animals he had never seen glared down from the limestone walls. He shuddered and hurried back. His mission was done.

After a time he washed in the brooklet and scraped the mud from his clothing. He was interrupted by a sound. The eerie whistle! He darted to the entrance. Quara was coming up the trail, two large packs on his shoulders. He eased them down before the cave. "The forest is clear."

"That whistle!"

"Whistle?" Quara laughed. "Do you mean this?" From his pouch he drew a long piece of staghorn. Two small holes were cut on one side.

The stranger put it to his mouth and blew. A piercing shriek filled the cave. Arvi jumped. "Stop!"

"It is only my flute," Quara said. "I can imitate birds and can play softer melodies, too."

"That was a frightening sound,' said Arvi in awe. "Every time I have heard it, it has meant trouble."

"I can see why." Quara scowled. "I intended to warn you when I blew it.

"Many days ago I fell in with Warth and his men, hoping to trade with them. In my own language my name, Quara, means 'The Trading One.' I travel from land to land to barter or trade the trinkets in my pack. I carry the products of many lands.

"But I made a mistake in trying to trade with those you call 'The Shining Stones.' When I met them they were on their way to raid your village. They took me prisoner, so that I could not go ahead and warn anyone."

Arvi said, "You are lucky that they didn't kill you."

"They didn't dare." Quara smiled grimly. "Warth knows the strength of my tribe in the Land of the North, and he knows also that if he slew me, my brothers would seek revenge. Besides, Warth fears that I carry magic in my packs."

"Magic!" Arvi exclaimed.

"Little figures made by the medicine men of a strange land. Warth waited nearby until your harvest was nearly complete. He thought to slay you while you worked in the fields. He and his men were watching all the time!"

The boy shivered. "I thought there were just one or two—"

"They were all there. Then I approached Warth and offered to call upon the spirits to help him: I played very loudly on the flute. The sound did what I hoped it would. It frightened you. You got away."

Quara's eyes sparkled. "That knife you threw just missed Warth. And I never saw anyone run as you did! You outflew the arrow he shot! Warth was in a rage. Save for my magic he would have slain me on the spot!"

"It is well that you got away, and that you still have your packs," Arvi said.

"I hid them during the attack. While everyone else was storming the fence, I took a chance and flung them into a tree. Then I blew another warning on the flute."

"We heard that," Arvi recalled. "If our battle chieftain had taken the first warning, we might have been better able to defend ourselves. But he didn't." He told Quara about the council.

Quara listened closely. "Your people would be strong enough to throw back the Shining Stones if they would work together."

He looked down at Arvi. "What about those two jars?"

"I may not say."

"They seemed important," Quara said.

When the boy said "They were," Quara stared reflectively. Then he picked up his packs. "Back to the village. And I am going with you."

The dugout was safe, but Quara said, "We must make very sure that we are still alone. We can see most of the lake from here. We will watch for a few more moments before we venture into the open." From a pack he took some meat, handed a large piece to Arvi, and sat down. They ate in silence. When Quara was sure that they were not being watched, they paddled across the river and tied the dugout near the swamp trail. As they hurried along, Quara became more alert with every step; near the village he set his packs in a high tree. Arvi found his heart thudding. What would they find? Were the people safe? And why were there no sounds or voices?

The air was thick with smoke as they came to the clearing. No one was in sight. Arvi gasped. The palisade was flat. Where the long houses had stood were oblongs of blackened stones. The granary stood empty.

Quara poked among the ashes. "Everything has been dug up and carried away from its hiding place. Warth's victory was complete."

"Where are Lani and Hawk!" cried Arvi.

"Don't call. The enemy may be near," Quara warned.

Then a voice said, "Stand!" Trotting Fox, Foxhead, and Cub Fox strode from the forest, arrows ready. "The tall one must be a Shining Stone," Foxhead was saying.

The three hunters were grimy from the battle. Trotting Fox had an ugly wound on one shoulder. He looked uncertainly at Arvi. "Did you run away?"

"I did not run to save myself," the boy replied.

As the hunter looked doubtful, Quara said, "You need not aim arrows at us. I am not a Shining Stone. I am a

44

trader. And in my tribe we would not question a chieftain's son as you do."

"Chieftain's son!" the hunter snorted. "Hawk is not a chieftain here." As his brothers covered him with their weapons, he grabbed Quara's javelin and flung it aside. "Hawk has run away. If there is a leader, I am he!"

Arvi Keeps His Secret

THE HUNTERS shoved Quara to the ground and quickly bound him hand and foot. Arvi was too dazed to protest; Cub Fox jostled him with his spear, keeping him away, as the older brothers whispered together and then hurried away to the forest. Cub was left as guard.

"Go over to the council place," Cub Fox said. "We must send up a smoke signal, for the people may now come in safely."

Arvi said, "Tell me, Cub, where are my people?"

"Hawk fled, as my brother told you. Lani and Londa escaped, for when the stockade fell, the women and small children fled to the fishing raft and pushed themselves out onto the lake. The men and older boys fought and retreated into the swamps.

"Now take my cloak, Arvi, and hold it over the smoke

for signals!" Cub watched closely, his spear threatening.

Arvi obeyed. The smoke puffed high over the desolate clearing. "It is enough," he said after a while, but Cub Fox told him to keep on. Over the youth's shoulder Arvi saw Quara nod at the cloak. Arvi understood.

He turned as if to wave the cloak but instead whipped it across the spearhead and flung himself upon Cub, who yelled and stumbled back. Arvi struck out with his fist. Cub gasped and lay stunned.

Arvi grabbed the spear and ran to untie Quara. "The little fox was outwitted—and outfought." The trader chuckled.

"He groans," Arvi observed, "but he is only stunned. Now we must find Lani and Londa. They must have seen the signals."

"And I must get my packs," Quara said, "for I will be safer here when people see what I bring." He bounded away. Cub Fox sat up, grumbling but making no other move, as Arvi hurried to the lake shore. From the cove where it had been sheltered, the raft was now being poled across the water. Lani and Londa were in the throng, waving

and shouting eagerly to Arvi.

From the raft the homeless ones stumbled to the beach to stare in horror at their burned village, to wander through the ruins and rummage in the ashes. Others came from the swamps, passing Arvi with hardly a glance; they were too intent upon their own misery. There were none who had not lost their homes, their tools, food, and live-stock—the things that kept them alive in the wilderness. Almost everything that had not been stolen had been burned and spoiled. The more dreadful news came out as the people milled around: men had been slain, and Shomu and Hawk were missing—perhaps dead. Many defenders had

48

been wounded, or scarred in fighting the fires.

With Hawk gone, the belief grew that the village would be abandoned and a camp set up in the marshland. The hunters wanted that, saying they would not live in the open lest the Shining Stones return.

Lani was relieved to find that Arvi was safe. But her face showed her concern for Calling Hawk. "He is missing," she admitted. "But he would not have fled."

"He fought bravely," Londa said. "Bending Branch saw him leap from the palisade to attack the enemy who had the battering ram." She asked Arvi how he had escaped, but the boy could not explain fully and keep his

49

promise; he told briefly of Quara's aid, and Lani and Londa seemed satisfied and pressed him no further.

Looking through the throng for a sight of Quara, Arvi saw him when he came from the swamp trail. When Arvi pointed him out, Lani said, "Go to him. Ask him to stay here with us before something happens to him. Quickly, for the men are still on edge. One might send an arrow at him, for he is a stranger to all but you."

Arvi ran to Quara and repeated what Lani had said. And remembering Trotting Fox, the trader agreed. Packs in hand, he stood close to the family as the men gathered.

They were a weary and battle-torn group, their clothing ragged, their weapons broken, their manner showing their discouragement. Towards Quara there was suspicion. For Arvi there were scowls and dark glances, because the story of his flight had been passed along much as Cub Fox had started it; none know—or could be told—Arvi's reasons. Arvi thought of Shomu, wondering if the One of Wisdom would appear and say a word in his defense. But there had been no sign of Shomu since the battle.

Quara did not wait long to begin his trading. He suddenly spoke in a loud voice: "Is there a fisherman here, one who earns his living from the lake?"

Snapping Fish asked, "Who is that fellow?"

Someone else growled, "Does he think we live near a lake and do not fish?"

"I would talk with a good fisherman," Quara persisted, "one who knows the value of a fine hook and would trade for it."

"I am that one," Snapping Fish said; "but every hook and line I had was burned in the fire."

Quara held up his hand. "This hook bears a charm so that even the sly pickerel cannot pass it by. And once caught, the fish cannot escape, though he leap and thrash the water to a boil."

The fisherman's eyes bulged. "Hold it still. Let me see it. Why, it is well carved and sharp as a sliver."

"I would trade it. And I have others, equally enchanted, that will take perch, salmon, carp, and herring."

"I have an otter fur that the enemy did not find."

"This many hooks for the skin." Quara put several into the man's hand. Other men crowded closer. "Ax heads

of hardest stone." Quara held up a pair. "They get sharper as they are used. Here are adzes, scrapers, fire-flints, and knife blades of green stone!"

Suddenly Trotting Fox burst into the crowd. "I captured you once," he roared at Quara. "Who freed you? Where is Cub?"

"Cub holds his head in his hands," Quara said. "A lad younger than he gave him such a blow that he is still dazed."

52

The hunter reddened. "Move over here where we can see you. You came with the enemy. You will be tried—"

"I am willing that the men try me. They will know I do not resemble the enemy." Quara dragged his packs to the council area. Trotting Fox followed suspiciously.

"This man was in league with the Shining Stones," Trotting Fox said to the men. "The stranger should be slain. And the boy—"

"If I were in league with Warth, I should have fled long before this," snapped Quara. "I stayed here to trade with the villagers. That is my way." He turned around so that all might see. "Those of you who came close enough to the enemy to know—do I look like one of them?"

"He does not," Bending Branch whispered. "What a tall, lanky fellow!"

"He wears almost no beard," Ruru observed, "and he is very blond. I wonder how he gets his beard shaved, whether he plucks it, which hurts mightily, or scrapes it down with a knife or the edges of broken pottery—"

Trotting Fox insisted, "He was with the Shining Stones. His javelin has a shiny point—"

"I seized it from one of the enemy," Quara retorted. "Others did the same. There are many weapons like it in this gathering." This was true; a murmur of doubt ran around the circle.

"If you are not a Shining Stone, then who are you?" Grebe called, "and why were you with them?"

"I am Quara, the Trading One. Many languages do I speak, but my own is that of the Land of Many Snows. I am far from my homeland now, for my trading leads me from land to land to the villages of many tribes. As a trader I bring the riches of one land to the folk of another, in exchange and barter."

Quara reached into one of his packs. "Here are rich dyes of red and yellow ochre; hairpins of carved bone; combs of yew wood; pendants and bracelets of boar's teeth; rings for the ears or nose; beads of amber.

"Here is asphalt for gluing the blade and handle of a knife—" Someone shouted in eagerness, but Trotting Fox glared him into silence as the trader went on.

"Lengths of linen string that are stronger than cedar fiber; buttons and needles; clay sinkers for fish nets—"

Grebe muttered, "I have made many of the things he has, but I have never heard anyone talk as he can."

"Here are eagle feathers for fletching arrows, so charmed that the arrow shaft wings after the prey; here are wooden bowls, hooks for hanging clothes." Quara paused at last. "All these will I trade, or exchange for food and lodging.

"Trotting Fox, when my supplies are gone, I will go away, and one day return with whatever the people want me to bring."

The hunting chief was hesitant. But Bending Branch said, "We need those adzes and ax-heads at once if we are to build again, for they take as long to make as the beams of a house. I cannot wait. Indeed, I could have my house framed while others are still trying to replace the tools they lost in the battle."

Several men applauded, and there was a rush towards the trader. Many held up the few things they had salvaged from the ashes; all wanted to trade, or to get promises of new tools from Quara on his next trip.

Trotting Fox brooded as the stranger went on trading.

55

"You do well with the people," he admitted. "They are sorely in need of these things. I will not interfere; you are free to come and go as you please. Now those eagle feathers—"

"I will bring more to exchange for a necklace of fox paws such as you wear," said Quara quickly. The chief nodded.

"Get on with the council," Woran said. "Night comes, and we have no shelters. We can trade later."

"The boy," said Foxhead. "He ran from the battle. He carried something, perhaps food that his father wanted to save. It is not right for some to hoard food while others have nothing."

There was a sudden hush. "It is well for you that Hawk is not here." Bending Branch stood up. "If he were, he could answer you. But I will not attend a council where a warrior may not speak for himself."

"Hawk seems to have run away," Trotting Fox said. "But the boy should speak."

Arvi felt the eyes of the men on him. "When I ran I was under orders from Shomu and Hawk—"

56

"The One of Wisdom is not here," someone said. "It is feared that he lies wounded or slain in the wilderness."

"What were the orders?" asked Trotting Fox quietly.

The youth stared at the ground. "I may not say."

"You had better speak, for you are being tried," Ruru warned him. "Now I can think of but one reason—"

Arvi's eyes widened. He looked fearfully at Ruru the farmer. In desperation he shook his head. If Ruru knew or guessed—"I may not say," he repeated.

A babble of talk arose. Quara interrupted. "I saw him risk his life; he had a mission to fulfill and would let no one stop him. Indeed, when I met him and tried to halt him to ask his help in escaping the Shining Stones, he mistook me for one of them and tried to battle with me! He does not lack for courage nor a sense of duty."

Trotting Fox cut him off. "You are not one of us, Quara, and your vote may not be counted in the council."

"Arvi is one of you and deserves more thanks than he is getting," the trader shot back. "He did as his orders told. That is more than can be said for another." He pointed to the one he meant.

Trotting Fox suddenly turned on his younger brother and cuffed him soundly with the back of his hand. And as the youth backed away, the chieftain roared, "He means you, Cub Fox, and some of what he says is true. You could not guard a lad younger than yourself. You disgrace a great family of warriors."

"Enough talk," Foxhead snapped. "Hawk is not here. We need a village chieftain in his stead. One man should take charge, as Shomu said. This is the time to vote for a chieftain."

The men agreed. Arvi walked away. Boys could attend some of the councils, but only the men could cast a vote. Further, he cared but little who their choice would be. The men would get around to his case, he knew, and until then he could do nothing. Quara picked up his packs and joined him on the far side of the village.

Neither of them was surprised a moment later when they heard a shout which proclaimed that the chieftain would be Trotting Fox. The men stayed in council for a little longer; then Trotting Fox stepped away from the circle and beckoned to Arvi.

"The men have spoken," he said. "For the time being, at least, I am chief.

"There is no final decision about you, because they do not know all the facts. Hawk is not here, and you refuse to speak.

"Now we are going away, to build a camp in the swamps." He looked beyond Arvi to where Lani and Londa waited near the ruins of their dwelling. "Your family may come with us, though there are some people who distrust them because of the strange way that Hawk disappeared and because of your actions.

"But if you do come, Arvi, you may not attend the councils and you may not hunt or fight with us. Thus will it be until we know more about why all these things happened." Trotting Fox stalked away.

Arvi told Lani what the chieftain had said. Her reply was quick. "They do not want us. We will stay here."

A Message from Hawk

BEFORE NIGHTFALL the village was nearly deserted; the people had quickly divided among themselves most of the logs of the old palisade and had carried them away to use for building anew in the marshland. Lani and her family were allowed their share, and with Quara's help, a lean-to was put up. Londa brought in reeds for thatching a roof; Arvi daubed the sides with clay.

Bending Branch paused at the lean-to. "You would be wise to come with us," he told Lani. "This place is not safe. Don't you remember Shomu's prophecy? The smoke went low over the village—a bad sign."

"The smoke went also to the marshes," Lani reminded him. "Shomu said the Evil Spirits were there, too. He may have meant the vipers and adders that crawl in the deep grass, and the mosquitoes which fly in clouds.

"But that is not the real reason we will not go. Trotting Fox does not want Arvi there. The boy would be scorned. Therefore we shall stay here. We shall be alone for a while, but Hawk will return. We'll wait here for him."

The carpenter shook his head doubtfully. "He may never return."

When Bending Branch had gone, Quara said, "He may be right, Lani. Remember, too, that with the palisade gone this clearing will be open to wild animals. Wolves, bears, and wild boar will venture close at night. And I cannot stay here for very long. You will have only Arvi to drive them away.

"The swamp is not good, but Trotting Fox is right in going there for a time. The people can hide from robbers; they can hunt, or fish in the river. It is safer than the mountains, where avalanches are a danger. And it is better than leaving now for a new home in the lowlands, for when snow comes, travel will be difficult."

"Long before that," Londa pointed out. "The mountain passes are blocked with snow before it snows here."

Quara was surprised. "The passes to the south also?"

"Yes," said Lani. "Snow comes early there. Indeed, one cannot leave the lake country at all after the last moon of summer."

"Then I must go away sooner than I expected. You must make plans: you need weapons and tools; you need traps, snares, fish nets and lines—"

"Londa will help me," Lani replied. "We can find berries, roots, and some vegetables—"

"All those, and more, if you are to survive," Quara declared. "It is a bleak outlook."

"Bending Branch alarmed me with his gloomy talk," Arvi said. "Now you make it worse!"

The trader eyed his packs as if he were counting the things that remained. "I can stay for a few days."

Lani began a net at once with a ball of cord that Quara had. Londa scraped away at strips of cedar bark, preparing the fiber for string when the cord ran out. And Quara and Arvi worked until late on their weapons—stout bows of yew and straight, deadly arrows.

When the moon was high the family huddled together in the rough shelter, and Quara made himself a sleeping

62

place at the entrance. Leaning against the logs, he set his javelin across his knees. From a pack he took the little flute; this time there was no shrieking whistle, but music, low, soft, and plaintive. The melodies were strange.

Presently Quara put the instrument away. In the flickering light he seemed once again the shadowy stranger of the night before. Arvi remembered the long arms that had reached out at him, and he shivered. He glanced out at the silent figure; the leather helmet was tipped low over the man's forehead, but the sharp eyes stared as bright as sparks into the darkness.

The next morning Arvi and Quara made a pitfall large enough to trap a small deer. Near the lake they set snares for birds. The next day they finished the net and made fish traps like wicker baskets. Because Hawk had devised the raft and had built it, with some help from Bending Branch, Arvi felt that it belonged to his family. He spoke to Lani, and they agreed that even if the other people should want the well-cut logs and timbers, they should not be allowed to touch them.

Quara was doubtful of the value of the raft: the logs

would make a good beginning for a new palisade, he hinted. But neither Arvi nor Lani would consider using them. Even though a fence around the hut might take many, many days of hard labor, the raft must not be touched.

"When the sturgeon or herring run, we need the raft. Standing on it, we put ourselves over deep water," Arvi said.

Quara shrugged. "You have made your decision. But I cannot stay; when I have gone you will need a palisade even if you must go without food to get on with it!"

During the next few days they trapped a marten and several birds. The net was finished. Arvi and Londa sometimes brought in a catch large enough to leave the pebbly beach a squirming mass of silver.

At night they would build the fire high and Quara would tell stories of faraway lands and folk, or play again upon the flute.

But there came a morning at last when Arvi saw that the trader's sleeping place was empty; the packs had disappeared, and no one answered when Arvi called. "Quara has gone!" the youth exclaimed.

Lani seemed resigned. "He could not stay. He told

us that. He is as much a wanderer as a trader; he cannot stay in one place for very long. When winter has come and gone, he may return to trade with the people."

"The clearing seems more desolate than ever," Londa said.

Arvi agreed. "It is as if another fence were torn down. We shall have to be on our guard. Oh, I wish Hawk were back with us!"

But Lani would not speak further of their misfortunes. Instead she planned the day's work and kept her worry to herself. There was wood to gather, food to find, tools to make, and a palisade to build.

Arvi hurried away to tend his traps; a ruffed grouse and a pigeon were dangling in the nooses. After taking them and resetting the strings, he set out for home, more light-hearted than before. Part way he halted to examine some pawprints in a muddy place; they were bear tracks. He said nothing of this to Lani and Londa. But that night he built the fire closer to the lean-to.

The palisade grew slowly. Working alone while Lani and Londa scoured the countryside for food, Arvi cut many

saplings, but scores of them would be needed.

They had an unexpected visitor one day. Snapping Fish strode in; a smaller figure hobbled beside him. When Arvi saw who it was, he shouted. "Shomu!" Snapping Fish explained. "He came back several days ago, weak and feverish with hunger. Now that he can walk again, he wishes to speak to you."

"What of Hawk?" Arvi asked eagerly. "Was he with you?"

Shomu motioned to everyone that he wanted to talk with the boy alone.

"The seed?"

"I won't," Arvi said. "I have faced the scorn of the hunters for so long that I do not mind now. All I care about is Hawk—when will they release him?"

"They would not say that they would ever release him," Shomu answered. "He is a wise man and a good hunter; sometimes they adopt one of their enemies to replace some favorite of their own who has been slain."

Lani and the others came close. They heard Shomu say, "Hawk is safe, so long as none try to follow and set him free."

"Quara!" Londa gasped. "He might try!"

"He was going off on a trading trip—" Lani began. "But he asked of the mountain passes to the south. That is where the Shining Stones live, isn't it, beyond the farthest mountains to the south?"

They stared at each other; their first relief on hearing of Hawk was gone; a new fear had arisen.

"Who is Quara?" the old man quavered.

Lani described him and told of his aid and his warning to the village.

"The Spirit of the Night Birds warned us," Shomu said.

68

"If he carries the magic of the Night Birds in that whistling flute, then he carries a great magic indeed—he may be safe."

Snapping Fish asked, "What of the rest of the prophecy?"

"I evoked the pictures in the smoke. But while I know many things, I do not always see the explanations of the magic. I cannot answer, Snapping Fish."

He got to his feet. "There is still trouble with our people. They are many hunters, many farmers, many fishermen, but very few who work for the good of all. Therein lies the reason for our troubles. We cannot blame everything on the enemy."

"Now, that is the truth!" Snapping Fish exclaimed. "No hunters will help the fisherman when there is a run of sturgeon; if all were fishermen when there was a run, we could bring in a huge catch!"

"None ever helped the farmers in clearing fields or in other heavy work," Lani remembered. "Too many had excuses to offer instead of aid in building the palisade. So it fell."

"And so the village fell," Shomu declared. "Hawk is

the only one I know who has seen this all along and who has the leadership to command respect. I wish he were here."

Snapping Fish said, "Many would vote for him that hesitated before. Trotting Fox makes too many mistakes, and he does not seem to want his command now that he has it."

They talked long of affairs in the new camp. After a lingering and envious glance at Hawk's fishing raft, the fisherman escorted the older man away.

"A word from Shomu would free you from your promise and give you the respect of everyone in the village," Londa said to Arvi. "They would be glad to take us in with them."

"From the way Snapping Fish talked, the people quarrel," Lani reminded her. "They are more divided than ever. We are just as well off here. Further, the hunters may soon put themselves and everyone else in such a plight that they will finally turn to Hawk for help." She stopped, as if she had changed her mind about speaking on.

Arvi guessed what she would have said: "They will finally turn to Hawk for help—when, or if, he returns."

70

That afternoon a mist shrouded the mountains; a soft rain sizzled into the fire and into the embers under the smoking racks where the fish were being dried and cured. Arvi put more wood on, but the damp logs burned poorly; at dusk it appeared that both fires might soon go out.

The rain increased. Darkness fell. A cold wind rushed in from the lake. Beyond the orange fire there was only the still forest. No children called as they had in former times. No dogs barked; no goats stamped in their pens; no hunters marched in to throw down their burdens and sing in triumph.

Later, Arvi awoke. He wondered what had disturbed him; the rain had stopped. Then he heard a shuffling sound. From behind the lean-to came a sharp, splintering crack.

"What—what was that?" Londa and Lani cried. Arvi grabbed his bow and arrows.

"Don't go out," Lani warned.

"Someone—or something—is at the drying rack." Arvi motioned to Londa. "Take a spear."

"Don't!" Lani began. There was another cracking, and a heavy weight thudded against the rear wall. Arvi bounded out, with Lani and Londa close behind him. The lean-to trembled as if a giant hand had seized it. Arvi's bow twanged.

"It's a bear!" he gasped.

Londa clung to his arm. "Watch out—there are others!"

He yanked his arm free. "Throw the spear!" Londa raised it with shaking hands and hurled it wildly. A roar came at them.

"Run—run," Lani shouted. She threw a burning stick. It caught one of the animals full in the face. A roar shook the night. Londa sped towards the beach. Arvi ran several steps, then glanced back. Lani stood alone. He knelt, took careful aim, and shot past her.

Lani fled towards him. "We can't stay here. Get away —run to the raft. There may be others, and wolves may come in, for there will be the scent of death."

Arvi remembered the tracks he had seen. Lani was right. Others could be close by. He backed away, as the others gained the raft. "Loosen the ropes!" Londa called. Arvi leaped after them as Lani struggled with the knots.

72

"That's the last rope—push us away!" Lani said. "Hurry!"

Arvi dropped his bow and gave the raft a shove. It was so dark that he could not see Londa as she plunged in on the far side of the raft to help him. In another moment the heavy raft lurched free. Quickly they clambered onto the deck. They stared back to where the little fire still glowed.

The lake was deadly quiet. "It starts to rain," Londa whispered. They huddled together as the wind caught the raft and drove it slowly out into the blackness. "The storage shelter will hold us," Lani said, groping her way across the deck. "Push those traps outside."

They clung together in the little shelter as the storm raged on.

A Home on the Raft

AT DAYLIGHT the rain ended, and they came from the storage hut to see that the raft was lying across from the inlet of Black River.

"We are grounded on a sand bar," Arvi said. He started towards the edge of the raft, and it teetered suddenly.

"Wait—don't loosen it!" Lani scanned the wooded shore line. "We are not far from the lean-to. This is a good place to leave the raft. We might have to run to it again!"

"If there were a way to make a fire, we could just stay here." Arvi peered into the hut. "This is too small, though, and it is drafty and leaky. The rain dripped on my feet."

Londa said, "I don't know which was worse, fighting the animals or hiding here in the storm. I heard the howls of the Lake Spirits in the cry of the wind."

Arvi quoted Shomu: "Evil Spirits cannot reach across the water."

Lani said, "That part of the prophecy is explained. The bears could not reach us out here, nor could any other wild animal. Twice we have saved ourselves by fleeing to the raft. I think we would do well to stay here."

"We are almost out of bowshot." Arvi gauged the distance. "If we could get the raft a little farther out and tie it up somehow, it would be the safest place I can think of."

He tried an arrow. It arched up towards the shore and fell short. "The Shining Stones might be able to shoot farther than that," Londa said.

"The lake is large enough," Arvi pointed out. "But the sandbar ends here. We could work out some kind of anchor, if we had some help."

"Snapping Fish," Londa suggested.

"He would know how, and so would Bending Branch." Arvi climbed over the side. "We should go back to the lean-to. The bears are dead. We can have a feast on the meat!"

Lani and Londa followed him cautiously to the village.

The bears lay beside the lean-to. It sagged where one of the animals had tumbled onto it from the drying rack.

75

Londa groaned. "They ate most of the fish!"

"No matter." Arvi grabbed one of the animals by the ears and hoisted its head. The grinning mouth showed a row of long fangs. "That spear in its heart is yours!" Arvi said to Londa.

Lani shuddered. "It was a brave fight. Now let us move to the raft. We can take the skins and meat."

They needed a way to get to the raft easily, and as his mother and sister gathered their belongings and started to skin the bears, Arvi dragged saplings down to the beach. These he had cut for a palisade, but the need now was for a small raft to ferry them back and forth to their new home. He laced the logs together with vines.

Later he saw a dugout turn from the inlet. It was Snapping Fish's boat.

Arvi waved. "We need help."

Snapping Fish jumped ashore. "You seem to need a lot of help. Those vines must be tighter." He looked at the bearskins. "What happened?"

Arvi described the fight and the fisherman scowled. "There is evil in this place!"

76

"The camp is no better, from your own story of yesterday," the boy said.

"That is the truth! This morning I quarreled with the chieftain. I wanted to fish today, for I have had dreams of sturgeon as big as a man, churning the water to foam. I told Trotting Fox, but he laughed."

He scowled darkly. "In that camp all they have to eat now is meat, and snails from the mud. Oh, I would taste again the delicate flavor of broiled sturgeon!"

The fisherman sighed as he tightened the vines. Arvi told of their plan to move. "You are forced to go; it is the only thing you can do," Snapping Fish agreed.

"As you say, there may be a way to secure the raft. I'll ask Bending Branch. Look for us tomorrow."

The next morning the carpenter came in the canoe with Snapping Fish. After some discussion, the two men shoved the raft away from the sand bar and poled it farther out.

Bending Branch selected some thick logs from those Arvi had cut. Standing on the deck, the two men pushed logs straight down at the four corners of the raft. When only the tops showed above water, Bending Branch wedged

77

them to the raft beams.

"Now nothing, not the wind or waves, or even the winter ice, will ever wrench this raft from its place," the carpenter declared.

Lani thanked the men and gave each one a gift of bear meat. "You may come out here for your fishing whenever you choose," she said.

For several more days the family labored on the storage hut, enlarging it to hold their supplies and sealing it tighter with clay and mud. They built a hearth of flat sandstone. Next they began a rail and a fence around the raft: winter was not far away, and the raft must be protected against wolves that might dare to cross the ice.

Frost colored the trees. A film of ice formed over the lake; it melted before midday, but the family had its warning. Soon the country would be deep in snow. Arvi was ferrying firewood to the raft when he saw two figures hurrying along the southern shore. Were Bending Branch and Snapping Fish running from something? He stood up; the first figure was very tall—"Quara!" He felt his heart leap. "Quara, and Calling Hawk!"

Lani and Londa ran from the shelter. "Hawk!" Arvi shouted. "It is he—and Quara—there they are!"

Excitedly he cleared the raft to make room for his sister and mother and paddled towards the shore. Arvi and Londa howled in glee. But it was too much for Lani; huddled in a corner of the little raft, she bowed her head and wept.

Hawk greeted them affectionately, hugging his children as though he had never hoped to see them again; with an arm around Lani he listened more soberly as they tried to tell all that had happened, and as they asked of his own escape. Quara perched on a stump nearby, watching solemnly as Hawk told his story.

Hawk had tried to lead an attack on the battering ram. But the gate had broken, the enemy had swarmed in from all sides, and he had been captured. Soon after, Shomu, too, was taken.

"Warth said at first that I would be freed when his party had gained the last mountain pass to the south, if none of our men followed. But when we neared the pass, Warth changed his mind and ordered me to stay with him.

"But there was one who trailed us, though the Shining Stones did not know it," Hawk continued. "That was Quara. He must have traveled on wings, for he caught up with us three days before we were to reach the pass. Having found us, he followed and each night lay in wait near our camp, hoping for a chance to release me. His chance came when Warth prepared an attack on another village.

"As the Shining Stones held a war dance, Quara crept through the underbrush, cut the ropes which bound me, and thrust weapons into my hands. We ran.

80

"Warth saw us. One of his arrows wounded Quara, but he went on; he had made careful plans. He went straight to the village Warth had thought to raid. As we drew close, Quara took out a whistle and blew upon it. It was the same we had heard before; it sounded as if all the evil spirits in the world were clamoring and shrieking at once.

"The warriors of the village heard the warning. They rushed from their camp, waving weapons and shouting. Warth could chase us no farther, for he was well occupied!"

"We are overjoyed that you are safe," Lani exclaimed.

"Safe for a time, because the passes are now deep in snow; the Shining Stones are in their own land and cannot get through. But they will return just as surely as summer; they will come again and again until they are either slain or so defeated in battle that they will not dare to molest us."

Quara stood up restlessly. "Warth recognized me and roared that he would some day find and slay me."

Arvi shuddered. "I hope he never catches you!"

"I have outwitted him twice." Quara touched a scar on his shoulder. "But I have yet to pay him back for this. We shall see when the time comes."

There was a feast on the raft that night. Londa and Lani roasted some bear meat. Afterwards they sang and danced as Quara played merry tunes on the flute.

North winds whistled across the lake the next day. Hawk needed no other reminder of the season; plans must be made, and speedily. Brooding on the problem of a safe place to live, he paced the deck of the raft; his deep-set eyes scanned the shores, the white-topped mountains, the blue expanse of water rimmed now with the red and orange of autumn.

He studied the stakes which held the raft fast. "Whose work is this?" he asked Arvi.

"Bending Branch did it, with the help of Snapping Fish. They have been out here several times."

"And you thought to stay here all winter?"

Arvi answered, "We had no other place. Trotting Fox scorned us so that we were not welcome in the swamp camp; the lean-to was not safe."

Hawk looked over the side again. The rail and fence were still not finished, but he could see that Arvi had set them so close to the edges that there would be no foothold for anyone who attempted to storm the raft. He took his bow and an arrow, and said, "There is but one more question—"

"I do not think you can shoot to the shore," Arvi told him. "We thought of that, too: the raft is out of bowshot and none can reach us here without showing himself."

Hawk's burly arm drew the bow nearly double, and the string twanged hard. The arrow splashed offshore. "You and Lani planned well. I made plans during the days when I was captive. But this seems to be better."

Hawk Builds a Fortress

THERE WERE visitors to the lake dwelling that day. Snapping Fish had come to fish and had seen Hawk, and the news spread swiftly. Bending Branch and Ruru hastened to greet the chieftain and hear of his adventures.

"Everyone will rejoice to see you," Ruru told Hawk, "but unless you have a new plan that will safeguard them, none will want to return here. Even then it would be difficult to persuade some to come back, because they fear that the place is full of evil spirits."

"I had a plan," Hawk answered. "I thought to rebuild the village with a stronger palisade.

"But there is a better plan now. It is not as difficult, and if I could get enough men to join me, we could fight off the robber bands that plague us and never be defeated again." He pointed to the raft. "We will build a fortress right here."

"It is safe, as you and Hawk commanded."

Shomu sighed. "I wanted to be sure."

"And Calling Hawk?" Arvi begged. "What of him?"

"They took him prisoner. Later they captured me, also, and took me with them. They soon released me, so that I could take a message to Trotting Fox.

"This was the message: Hawk is alive, but is to be held as a hostage against pursuit. The Shining Stones were heavily burdened with their loot and could travel but slowly. They feared that Trotting Fox might speed ahead and lay an ambush. Therefore, if anyone attempted to follow Warth, Hawk was to be slain." Shomu's voice trembled. "When they set me free they left me no food, and I was too weak to travel fast. Finally some of our hunters found me. I have been sick, or I would have seen you before."

Arvi was bitter. "And would no one come here and tell us that Hawk was safe?"

Shomu replied, "I wouldn't tell them! You are the first to hear it." And as Arvi shouted "Hawk is safe!" to Lani and Londa, the old man said hastily, "Tell what you want of the capture. But nothing of your own mission."

"In the water?" Ruru gaped. "It could not be done!"

Hawk shrugged. "It is partly done, even now. When I was away, my family lived here in comfort, while you ran from snakes and were eaten by insects in the swamps. Where did most of the people go during the battle? Where did Lani, Londa, and Arvi go when the bears threatened them, and when the folk in the swamp scorned them?"

"To this raft." Ruru backed away under Hawk's fiery gaze. "But one could not live on the water—"

Quara interrupted. "Oh, one could. Indeed, I have seen people live in all sorts of places: in caves, in tents, in pit dwellings in the ground, in treetop houses, and in huts made of snow and ice! One could live very well on a raft such as this."

"I could fish all the time," Snapping Fish reflected.

"How would you get wood out here? Beneath all our weight, the raft would sink." Ruru was stubborn.

"The wood can be floated out," Hawk replied. "And if we had Bending Branch to help us, the lake village would be as solid as the ground itself."

The carpenter said, "The decks wouldn't sink, because

they would not be floating in the first place: they could be built upon logs driven into the lake bottom, as my house in the swamp is set over mud."

"Madness," Ruru muttered. "We would tumble into the lake. The fish would eat us."

Bending Branch tapped him impatiently on the shoulder to insist that if he planned the buildings they would not sink, and they went back towards shore. Quara spoke loudly, so that they could still hear: "I, for one, will help with the lake village, for I will thus assure myself a place of safety when I need it."

"Well spoken, Tall One!" Hawk chuckled grimly. "Your words will have meaning when all the other arguments have failed."

"I meant what I said," Quara declared. "Winter will not wait. The shores are rich with oak, beech, birch, and fir. Let us begin!"

So it was that they began. The fence around the deck was first. Next they started another shelter. Another raft would follow, and it would be set above the water and built solidly on many thick pilings. They hoped to continue even during the winter by preparing a great number of logs.

On shore, Hawk, Quara, and Arvi heaped the dry leaves of autumn close to the bases of many trees at once and set fires, hurrying from one trunk to the next, shouting in triumph as each new tree plunged down.

The other people saw what was happening. During the first month of work they came by in twos and threes to stand at a distance and argue, but to turn away.

Snapping Fish often watched as he fished, and he would offer his canoe for towing new logs out to the raft. Bending Branch, finishing a canoe of his own up on the bank of Black River, would pause to stare moodily at them, and would leave his work to give advice.

"Not like that," he would say. "Both ends should be charred first; they become easier to shape." Or he would sharpen Arvi's ax, or tell Quara how to cut a notch.

One day Hawk straightened up as if to rest his arms. "Your advice is excellent," he told the carpenter. "But you don't offer to follow us all the way."

The fisherman and several others were within hearing. Hawk spoke deliberately: "Your talk is good. You save us from making errors, for you know about carpentry and construction. But advice is not enough.

"We need the full co-operation of every one that can wield an ax. We need the strength of every man and boy." He pointed to where the piles for the new raft rose like a blackened, burned-out forest in the water. "Do you think that we could ever live together in that small place unless we give up some of our own plans and work for the common good?"

Bending Branch squirmed. "I have never heard you speak so coldly. You glare at me as if I were a stranger."

Hawk brushed his words aside. "Trotting Fox fancies himself a chieftain, but under him everyone does as he pleases. He goes off on his trips with Foxhead, Cub, and the others and leaves you without any leadership. You have no goats or cattle left from the raid, yet you find no others to tame. You have no grain, and you seek none. The fields need further clearing, and no one works them.

"Warth plans another raid next season, and all you plan is to run and hide." Hawk's voice rose, sharp as flint. "Now I say this to you and to the others that hear so that they may repeat it to the folk in the swamps: my fortress will be safe. But none save those who devote all their time and strength to it will ever set foot upon it.

"The robbers may burn you out of the country. Your cries may fill the air. But I will offer neither the strength of my spear nor the shelter of the raft unless you follow the plan, all the way!"

Bending Branch silently picked up his tools and turned slowly back towards the swamp trail. Lani said, "He walks away as though he had been whipped, Calling Hawk; you were harsh."

"I think of his life as well as ours."

Quara sighed. "You return, and all know that you

never ran away and never abandoned the fight. You are still chief in civil matters. You have Shomu's support. Still Trotting Fox does nothing. The council does not meet. Now Trotting Fox especially needs to be taught a lesson. You, Hawk, are the only one of the people who is as big and as fast with weapons as he is. You could force him to join us."

Arvi looked uneasily at his father. There was no hesitating in Hawk's reply. "I could force him. Indeed, I would slay him if I thought it would solve anything.

"But the kind of village we want can be built and held together with only one thing—that is, co-operation. For the lack of it the other village fell. If I used force now, I

should set a poor example. Further, the other men would not join in the labor with their whole heart and mind."

Quara said, "You may be right. If something goes wrong, those who were forced to join would be quick to blame you. But if they come of their own will, they will be more apt to take things as they come, without complaint."

"That is true. Remember Warth: he lives by force. He too, is strong, and he holds sway over his men with his fierceness. But what would happen to his tribe if he were to be slain?"

Hawk made steady progress. A second raft budded out from the first. Quara stayed on. His long arms wielded

his huge ax so well that he sometimes felled a score of trees in a single day.

Lani and Londa brought in stores of nuts; they made new jars, footed vessels to stand in rows, others with lugs on the sides so that they could hang from the rafters. Into the fresh clay they pressed the print of the food each contained. They stored wild carrots, fieldbeans, and parsnips along with baskets of dried apples, grapes, and dark plums. They cut a small hole in the floor of the new raft as it was built. Into this they could lower fish traps or sweep refuse.

But except for an occasional hedgehog or rabbit that Arvi trapped, there was little meat, and their supply of furs was not enough for winter clothing. They missed the hearty meals that meat could make, but above all they missed the grains. These had been staples in former days; they had been certain when meat and wild fruit were hard to find.

Hawk would recall the roasted barley meal, the bread and flat cakes of wheat made savory with poppy or caraway seed. Arvi would think of the jars of seed grain that he had hidden; he longed as the others did for an end to the toil and hunger.

92

At night and on stormy days they stayed secure in their new dwelling. Hawk would plan for the morrow: this or that grove of trees would be next, to afford no hiding place at that point for robbers. Or he would cut branches and twigs to make models of a dock or causeway.

The dock was difficult to plan. It would be needed when they kept goats or cattle: the animals could graze on shore in the daytime, but at night or in times of danger they should be tethered on the raft. Only a causeway that reached all the way would suffice, and if the animals trod it, so could the enemy.

They made a model of a runway, trying one idea after another. The simplest answer was the one that eluded them the longest. It was to make the pilings permanent, but to make them too far apart for a man to jump from one to the next. The beams and crosslogs could be made flat and not fastened at all. Thus, when they had to, they could retreat to the raft, picking up the logs and bringing them in as they came.

Winter on the Rafts

ONE MORNING a canoe sped from the inlet. "Bending Branch!" said Arvi. "His family is with him, and his canoe is loaded with gear!"

"He is the one we need most of all," Hawk muttered. "Do you suppose that he is giving in at last?"

They watched as the canoe was tied up to the gate at the rail. The carpenter held the craft as his wife and children climbed up.

He walked up to Hawk. "I would join you."

"On the terms that I laid down that day?"

"On those same terms. You have a plan. The others do not. We feasted there one day, and starved the next."

"I should tell you that we have but little set aside for the winter," Hawk said grimly. "You may not eat better here. We have placed the village first and our comfort second."

The carpenter said, "But you think ahead. The others do not. Now there are several who have figured out that when Arvi ran that time, he carried seed grain to hide. Indeed, they are so sure that that is true that they have tried to find the seed—"

Arvi gasped. "I never thought it would really be like that, though Shomu foresaw it." Hawk shook his head warningly, and the boy fell silent.

"They claim that a sack of wheat or even the poor-tasting millet would be enough for a few days. I do not know whether their guesswork is correct or not," Bending Branch went on. "I do not care. But they show they have even less sense than a squirrel, for the little animals know enough to set something aside!"

Hawk nodded gravely. "We must plan for every year, and not just for this one." He found Bending Branch a place on the newer raft, and because it was Hawk's way of doing things, everything else was stopped until the carpenter had a finished dwelling.

One morning someone saw that Black River was alive with a huge school of fish, leaping and thrashing into the lake. They seldom had seen anything like it at this season, and Hawk, knowing of their dangerously low reserves, ordered that everyone turn out to net as many fish as possible.

Snapping Fish, working all by himself, caught a good many fish. But when he saw the nets being hauled in to the raft, he paddled away, muttering to himself. He was gone only long enough to get his family and to gather his equipment. Then he headed for the lake village.

"None of the men in the other camp were on hand to take advantage of the run of fish," he told Hawk. "You had even the children at the nets and lines. That is as it should be. I see your method now. I am with you."

Hawk grinned. "We have enough fish to keep ourselves from starving for another moon. But what will Trotting Fox say?"

"I care not," the fisherman snapped. "He is seldom at hand to argue with. It may be days before he learns I am gone!"

Lani worried about Shomu. "If others leave the camp, who will care for him? He cannot hunt."

"I offered to bring him," Snapping Fish said. "But he feels that he should stay there. He says he is less of a burden in the camp than he would be here."

"We can take him," Hawk said briefly. "Tell him he would honor the new village if he lived in it. Tell him now!"

When the fisherman had gone, Lani said, "If Shomu comes, others will have new respect for this place."

"He will come," said the chieftain. "With the help we have gained, he can be provided for. He will know that."

97

Shomu came, just as Hawk had said; several others followed soon after. There was more help, but with it there were more demands on the stores of food. Hawk persisted with his work, driving everyone on to greater effort; through late autumn the men still cut new timbers.

But at last the winter blizzards howled across the lake country; the cold seeped like ice water through the chinks and cracks of the log dwellings.

One storm followed another; at times the people were bound to the rafts for days. Hawk worried. The jars of dried fruits and berries and the lines of smoked fish were emptied one by one. For a while they fished through the ice, until that froze so deep that they thought the lake had frozen all the way to the bottom.

Hawk wondered if he could hold his group through this season. Had things been any better in the swamps, he might have lost several families.

Quara refused to be locked in. He made a set of clumsy snowshoes from birch bark and strode across the ice and over drifts that could have swallowed even his tall figure. Arvi was much interested in the snowshoes: Quara made him a pair. Then, borrowing extra garments from Hawk and Lani, he dressed warmly and went with his friend to the shore.

In some of the windswept places there were prints of deer. "We could follow them if the snow wasn't so deep," the boy said.

"The snow may be in our favor," Quara remarked.

"Something draws them to this place," Arvi suggested.

Quara pointed upwards. "The ends of these tree branches are all chewed up. The deer are hungry, too, for the snows cover their usual feed. See where we cut the last few logs for the lake village—the deer have pawed away the snow to get at the bark!"

"If we could fell a tree—" began Arvi.

"We could lure the deer back. We could get them!" Roused by the thought of fresh meat, they hurried back to the village. Hawk joined them in their plan and they returned, heavily armed, to the shore.

Around the bases of several birches they kindled small fires, and when the trunks were deeply charred, they chopped the trees down quickly.

99

"The rest will not be so easy," Hawk warned. "We must wait—and we may not have a fire: that would frighten the deer. Remember, too, the deer may not come for several nights."

They drew away from the fallen trees; within bowshot they made a shelter in a windfall. All night through they waited in the numbing cold. At dawn they saw a herd of deer nibbling at the twigs.

"The drifts!" Hawk whispered. "Get behind the deer and the deep snow. Those we do not slay will founder." Slowly they worked their way around until they were in position. Then they loosed their arrows. Several deer fell. The rest bounded away, but the drifts slowed them down. Not one escaped.

It was a mighty triumph, and the villagers were busy for many days in cutting the meat, preparing the hides, and making robes and clothing.

100

Arvi Tells His Secret

THE WINTER moons passed slowly in the lake country, but there came a day at last when the ice cracked and
broke and when the birds returned to the forest.

On the morning after the first full moon of spring,
Shomu summoned Arvi and asked that the seed be brought
to the lake village. Hawk and Quara should attend as
guards. When they returned, Shomu would explain to
everyone.

Arvi led the way. So deep was the brooklet that they
barely got through with their torches. Inside the chamber
Quara exclaimed at the curious paintings. "It is a haunted
place," he muttered, and echoes whispered back "place—
place—"

"And there are arrowheads, shaped like laurel leaves.
They are far better than the gleaming stones that the enemy use."

Hawk was alarmed. "Don't touch anything. The men who once gathered here are gone, but their spirits remain. There is bad luck in these flints."

Quara took one of his own arrowheads, snapped it from its shaft, and placed it on the floor. Then he turned to Arvi. "The jars!" Arvi took them from the high ledge and passed them down, and the three hurried back to the lake village.

There was a festival that day. Shomu told of Arvi's courage and skill in evading the enemy and of his determination in keeping the secret.

The people applauded noisily. When Shomu had finished, they demanded that Arvi tell the story as he had experienced it; they yelled and stamped in excitement when they saw him act out the jump from the palisade, the run through the swamp, and the repulse of the enemy.

Then they marched to the planting fields, and with a great ceremony they lit a fire to drive away the Evil Spirits that might be there. The men cleared the planting space. And as was the custom, the women came after to sow and spread the seeds in the furrows.

102

When the ceremony was over, Quara said that soon he must go on his way; the trails were open, and he had many of a trader's promises to fulfill.

"You have made friends here," the chieftain told him. "You are a valiant warrior; there will always be room for you in our lake village."

The men each gave Quara an arrow for good fortune, and the tall man, after thanking everyone, placed the arrows in his quiver with his own. Arvi noticed that one of Quara's shafts had a curious head that differed from the rest: it was a flint carved like a laurel leaf.

During the summer the lake village slowly grew. Another platform branched out; pilings from three to nine inches thick and twenty or more feet long were cut, the largest for deepest water. Crosspieces were set over them, and these were covered with a floor of logs split in half. The spaces were packed with moss and clay until there was a solid base on which to build houses.

Like the older ones, the dwellings were rectangular, up to thirty feet long and twenty feet wide. The sides were branches woven together and plastered with clay. The

103

roofs were steep and thatched with grasses and reeds. Most houses had two rooms: one for cooking and eating, and another for sleeping. Outside were shelters for goats or other livestock and sheds for storage and workrooms.

When the folk in the swamp saw that the lake village was thriving, many more came to accept Hawk's terms. Ruru forgot his fears and brought his family also, but Trotting Fox and the hunters gave no sign that they would ever consider coming back.

As the first of the crops ripened, Hawk had a granary built. There was rejoicing when the first grain was harvested. Drums and rattles beat time for a dance. Hawk and his family were honored with many long speeches, but the chieftain had a sober word of advice: the harvest would amount to little if it were to be divided now; all of it should be saved for a better seeding in the spring. Shomu agreed with Hawk, and the decision was made as the chieftain recommended. Arvi was praised again for saving the seed grain, and the people remembered that some of Shomu's warnings and prophecies had come true.

"The smokes went low over the village: that was a sign of the fires," Ruru declared. "The smoke over the south meant that the Evil Spirits were there, and evil came from the south with the Shining Stones."

"The smoke over the trees told of the Spirits of the Night Birds and of their warning to us," Arvi said. "That may have meant the whistle that Quara brought."

Hawk suggested that the smoke over the lake meant the lake village and recalled that Shomu had said, "The Evil Spirits cannot reach across the water."

The One of Wisdom and Magic was called upon to speak once more. "Much of what was in the many smokes has come true," he said. "I caused the smoke to rise. I told you what I saw in the smoke pictures. But none can say what will really happen any more than he can describe the wind.

"One thing you have not mentioned: there was clearly a breath of many winds, which showed that the village was divided. It is still so. Some of our people have not come back to us. Trotting Fox and his men are brave hunters, and I shall have no peace in my heart until they are with us in this place."

The chieftain of the lake dwellers became more alert as the summer days went by. The harvest might once more be the signal for an attack by the Shining Stones, and Hawk resolved that this time there should be no surprise.

Some grain was left uncut for several extra days while the chieftain ordered that reserves of arrows and spears be made, that piles of stones for slings be brought in, and that lookout places be built and manned at every corner of the village. By delaying the final harvest, Hawk gained time

106

to arm; and if the Shining Stones were spying on the people, he delayed their attack also. Full well he knew that Warth was greedy and would not move until the riches of the village were ripe for the taking.

There came a day that was cloudy. Rain would spoil the grain, and Hawk could wait no longer. The women went to the fields under guard. The boys were sent to bring in the canoes and ferry rafts. At the lookouts men watched with bows in their hands, impatient for the return of the workers in the fields.

They came in at sundown with the rest of the grain. The logs on the causeway were rolled back to the rafts, and silence fell upon the lake shore.

"The Shining Stones may not come," Arvi said.

"They will come," said Hawk grimly. "Warth will never forget how I slipped through his hands. All winter long he feasted on grain while we were hungry. Robbing suits him well. He will try it again."

In the starlight, Arvi gazed at the shadow of the southern mountains. "He may be up there now."

"He is there, somewhere," Hawk said.

The Shining Stones Return

THERE WAS no attack that night. But Hawk would not give up his vigilance. Through days of waiting he paced the decks, spear in hand, scanning the shores. The people grew restless. This was the season for hunting, they complained. "You would be hunted, and not the animals," he answered. And at night he would awake to help those on guard, and to warn them that no sound must go unnoticed.

But it was not a sound which told that the enemy had come at least. One morning a thick black smoke rose over the swamps. From his lookout, Snapping Fish shouted. This could be a fire in the camp of Trotting Fox. Hastily Hawk called a council and checked his plans. When someone said that Trotting Fox was away and that his camp would be empty and unguarded, the men became worried. Could the few on the rafts turn back the Shining Stones?

"We shall turn them back," Hawk assured them. "Now we shall send a canoe along the shore of Black River to see if it is really the Shining Stones that we must fight. We shall go up to the edge of the swamp, and perhaps learn the strength of the enemy."

Hawk and two others left the lake village as everyone gathered to watch. Cautiously they glided along towards the inlet and entered at the widest place. They were gone but a short time, and when they returned, Hawk ordered the gates to be closed, and told the people what he had seen. The Shining Stones were in the swamps in great numbers. The hunters were indeed away, and only the old men, the women, and children left behind. These would not accept Hawk's advice to flee to the lake village. Instead they had gone into hiding in the vastness of the swamps and were now running before the wrath of Warth's men.

Even as Hawk spoke, a voice hailed him from the shore. The chieftain climbed to a lookout place. "It is Warth!"

Arvi saw the fierce chieftain for the first time. He was tall, dressed in robes of wolf furs, and his bearded face was

streaked with the paint of war.

"We have burned one village and will burn another," Warth was shouting, "unless you turn over your food and supplies to us. A giant tribute shall we take, for only thus can you appease our wrath for escaping us!"

"We shall give you nothing!"

Warth grew angry. "No tribe has ever defied me!"

"I defy you!" Calling Hawk brandished his spear.

"There is the first arrow!" someone whispered. "Warth himself has fired it!"

Hawk did not move. The shaft fell short, and a shout of gladness went up from the people. Hawk stepped down

110

from the high place. "Save your weapons. Loose not a single arrow until I command."

They waited as Warth and his men clustered together on the beach, waving their arms and pointing at the village. Then the enemy turned and vanished into the distant forest.

"What now?" Bending Branch exclaimed.

Hawk shrugged. "They await nightfall. Then they will try something else."

There was no other sign of the enemy during the afternoon.

"They may be making bark canoes, or a raft," Ruru said worriedly.

"We can drive them away, no matter what they do," Hawk said. "Flaming arrows of our own will light the lake and burn them from the water!"

Ruru's guess was right. After dark one of the guards saw a shadow on the water. "Wait until it is close," Hawk said. "They carry no fire. There is no real danger."

Hawk fitted an arrow to his bow. Around the tip he wound a bit of moss, lit it, and suddenly sent it flaming into the dark. All saw the canoe then. The arrow went true, and a score of others followed it. The canoe sank. The enemy swam away, yelling in alarm.

"So ends the second attack," Hawk said.

Bending Branch lowered his bow. "The lake village puts us on even terms with the enemy. We are few, but we are as strong as they!"

Hawk said, "Stronger. We shall win the victory!"

"Trotting Fox, Foxhead, and the others should be here," Snapping Fish declared. "With them we could hand Warth such a defeat that he would never return."

"When the hunters find out that their camp has been burned and their families driven away, they will come," Ruru said.

"They may not," replied Bending Branch. "Trotting Fox may do as he once threatened—lead his people to another place, far away."

"He must not!" exclaimed Hawk. "Call the men together. Put the older boys in their places as guards. We must plan some step right now."

The men came quickly to stand in a circle around the chieftain. "This village needs all its people," Hawk said

112

to them. "One of us must go to bring back the hunters."

"They are a day's march away," someone said. "They are in the Valley of the Sliding Snows."

"There is time," Hawk insisted. "Warth will stay, and we shall not give in. Now the hunters should be told again that the lake village is strong, that it holds under all attacks, and that they are welcome to join us. If Trotting Fox could hear what Snapping Fish said—that together we could break the strength of the Shining Stones forever—surely he would lead his men back."

"If he thought he had an even chance, he would welcome a fight," Ruru said.

"I would go and tell him," Snapping Fish said. "I know that hunting place in the valley."

"I did not intend to send a warrior," said Hawk. "But if the council approves, I will order Arvi to go."

Bending Branch grunted his approval. "He is fast. He could get through."

"He eluded the Shining Stones once before. He might do so again," Snapping Fish said.

Hawk hesitated. "Some doubted him that time. If

113

there is one who speaks against him, or who thinks the message would not be safe with him, I will ask another to go."

No one spoke.

Hawk dismissed the council. When he talked with Arvi his voice was tense. "You will be in great danger. But it is the wish not only of myself, but of everyone in the council that you be the one to seek out Trotting Fox and bring him back."

Arvi looked out at the dusk. "I would leave before the moon rises." Bending Branch and Snapping Fish were watching. He made up his mind to show no fear. "Tell me the place, and go over the message with me."

Hawk did. And when he had finished, Bending Branch said, "My canoe is the fastest. Take it to cross the lake, for when you gain the northeast shore, you are well away."

Soon Arvi was ready. Lani and Londa were pale and silent as they made up a small pack of food for him.

Snapping Fish thrust a quiver of arrows into the boy's hands. "The men offer these," he whispered. "They want you to use all their luck!"

114

Arvi slid down into the canoe and thanked Snapping Fish. "If you are not back in three days," Hawk told him, "I shall send someone else on your trail."

"I'll be back." The blade of his paddle touched the water noiselessly. The men closed the gate. All watched as the canoe vanished. A moment later Snapping Fish grabbed Hawk by the arm. "Look!" he hissed. "On the western shore!"

From the shadows another canoe slid forth. The lake dwellers lifted their bows. But near the raft the canoe veered northeast. Hawk's string twanged sharply.

"They are out of range," Snapping Fish muttered.

"They have seen Arvi," Hawk whispered. "Quick—take Bending Branch. Try to head them off!"

The two men ran to another canoe. "Get in—push us away—" They grasped the paddles and sped after the enemy.

"Faster!" Snapping Fish said. "They see us."

"Keep going." Bending Branch shot an arrow. Dark figures in the canoe ahead shot back.

"They think to cut us down and then go after the boy," the carpenter said.

"Turn around—let them see that we head for the raft. We can try to delay them so that Arvi can escape."

Bending Branch dropped his bow, and both men paddled desperately. The canoe bumped the pilings. They leaped out. Over their heads Hawk and the others loosed a cloud of arrows. The enemy canoe sped out of sight.

Hawk grasped the two warriors by the hand. "It was a brave deed. You delayed them. Arvi has a better chance." His voice was gruff. They hurried to their posts again and stared out across the lake. Over the edge of the mountains the moon rose bright and red.

116

A Mighty Victory

FAR OUT on the lake, Arvi heard the clamor as the Shining Stones came after him. He bent forward, muscles straining. Bending Branch and Snapping Fish had given him time and distance, but when he glanced back he saw that the gap was rapidly being closed. The enemy craft was manned by four men, and another was standing up waiting for a good shot.

The shore loomed up darkly. He flailed the paddle down. Someone shouted. A string twanged. Arvi ducked. The canoe hit the shore.

Arvi stumbled out. Arrows whipped over his head. Behind him there was a splashing.

Desperately he ran. He had no time to seek the trail; he went straight through tangles of underbrush. The men beat the bushes with their spears, seeking him.

On he sped. The land sloped, and Arvi nearly lost his balance, but he kept on running. The voices seemed fainter for a time, and he slowed to avoid tripping again. Then a voice echoed nearby, and footsteps crackled.

Panic ran through him; he started this way and that, then grabbed a tree branch and swung himself up. The footsteps hesitated, then thudded away.

He waited, nearly exhausted from his flight. There was more traveling to come, and he knew that he should rest. He climbed to a crotch in the tree and there bound himself with his belt as hunters sometimes did. After a long period of watching, he fell asleep.

At dawn the forest was still. Arvi untied himself and slid down quietly. Footprints were thick upon the ground: his enemies had passed and repassed this place in the dark.

Not far away he found the trail and started off. At midday he stopped to eat, then went on again. Far up in the mountains he came to the last pass before the Valley of the Sliding Snows. Opposite him were the white peaks where snow fell in thunderous avalanches. Below were the green meadows and a river.

118

At sunset he was in the valley; he turned from the trail to find a rock shelter that his people sometimes used. Along the stream there was a ledge; he dropped over. There, hidden on all sides, was a deep cleft under the ledge. He crawled in. There were the warm embers of a fire! Someone had stayed here. Was it the enemy?

He could not take a chance. Reluctantly he went back to the trail. He must find another shelter.

At last there was a smell of wood smoke. Cautiously he left the trail, searching, and finally saw the glow of a campfire. Beside it there was a familiar figure. "Trotting Fox!" he shouted.

The astonished hunters crowded around as Arvi gave them the message. The men exclaimed as they heard of the attack and prodded him for details. Those who had families in the swamp were in a rage.

"They should have accepted Hawk—they would be safe now," said Arvi. "He offered to take them in."

"We should all have accepted Hawk long ago," Grebe said bitterly. "Where can our families be now?"

"Twice the Shining Stones have burned my home,"

another hunter declared. "We should join Hawk. We could still hunt, and Trotting Fox would lead us. The difference would be that we would have to help—"

"I know Hawk's terms," Trotting Fox said.

"I would go at once!" Grebe said angrily. "We could fall upon the Shining Stones from the rear and crush them between ourselves and the lake dwellers."

A roar went up from the others. They brandished their spears and stamped in rage. Trotting Fox stepped back. "Wait—it may be too late—"

"We could go," Foxhead said suddenly. "If the raft is still standing when we get there, we could tear the Shining Stones to pieces. If the raft has fallen, then we will know that we should leave and never return."

Trotting Fox seized his weapons. "Break camp, quickly. We start tonight. If the raft is still safe, we will join the lake dwellers and fight with them."

The men greeted his words with a roar. Arvi reminded the chieftain of the enemy that had followed him, and of the warm embers he had found in the rock shelter.

"We will watch," the hunter said grimly. "In this place,

at least, we outnumber them." He gave the signal, and the group filed rapidly onto the trail.

They paused but briefly at the ledge. Finding no other signs, they went on. At dawn they climbed the last ridge, and Trotting Fox called a rest. Scouts circled on all sides, but they found nothing but a dead campfire and a single set of prints that no one recognized.

The march began again, through the pass and to the slopes that led to the lake country. In mid-afternoon someone shouted "Listen!" and they came to a halt.

Arvi felt a cold shiver down his back. "It is Quara's whistle!" he exclaimed.

The men hurried on towards the eerie whistling. It was suddenly silent, and they moved faster. Trotting Fox held up his hand to ward the men away and bent over the trail. "Four or five men passed here. See how the toes of the prints dig in—they were running."

"The same kind of prints I saw yesterday," Arvi said. "The Shining Stones must be after Quara. This is the time he was to return. The enemy that chased me has found him."

121

Trotting Fox broke into a fast run; the line of men thinned out. The two boys ran hard. Down the long slopes they raced until Arvi heard the chieftain's bellow: "There they are. They follow the Tall One. They may warn the others."

The hunters ran desperately. The Shining Stones had strung their bows to shoot at Quara. As Arvi caught up, he saw them and they saw the hunters. But before the enemy could change their aim, a storm of arrows whipped at them, and they fell.

Quara strode up; his eyes widened. "The Fleet One!" he said, breathing heavily. "You are safe!"

"Are there others near here?" Foxhead interrupted. "Quickly—how many were there?"

The trader answered that he had seen no others. Foxhead and his older brother talked briefly; they posted their group along the wooded fringe of the lake and crept away to scout the main force of the Shining Stones.

"Those that are slain are the ones that chased you," Quara told Arvi. "The day before yesterday I crossed a valley. I saw smoke and knew others were in this area. I tried to evade them; but their direction was the same as mine, and last night I found that I was again within sight of their campfire. I stole close and heard that they were roaming the hills to pick up your trail. I did not know where you were; indeed, I was not even certain that you were the one. It merely seemed likely when I heard their complaints of someone's ability to run!

"I decided to take them from your trail. I let them see me, and then led them a merry chase up and down the slopes. But they were fast and had nearly overtaken me when Trotting Fox burst in on them." Quara shook his head grimly. "These packs held me back. I should have hidden them!"

"You carry one arrow with a strange tip," Arvi said, his eyes on the trader's quiver. "If you took it from the Cave of the Ancient Ones—"

"You are going to say it is bad luck. I know that. But I left a stone of my own in the cave to appease the wrath of the Spirits. Soon I shall transfer the bad luck to the one that deserves it the most. Warth is at the lake shore now. I shall find him."

The scouts came back to report. Warth had built a raft with a fence in front; it was piled high with dry brush and was being moved from the inlet.

"The brushwood means fire," Trotting Fox declared. "Warth will have the raft poled out with his men crouching behind the palisade. When it nears the lake village, they will set fire to it and push it against the pilings. His men will jump overboard and swim back to shore."

"Stop them!" Arvi cried.

"We will. But we shall wait until those on the raft are over deep water. Then we ourselves shall set the raft to blazing, before the Shining Stones expect it!"

Quickly Trotting Fox gave his orders: to round the edge of the lake from the northeast and there to divide into two groups. One was to race down the beach; the other would fall upon the enemy from the rear.

As they drew closer, they slowed down to run more cautiously. "The lake village is quiet," Woran said as they came near.

"Hawk waits," Grebe whispered. "Warth has not won yet. If he had, he would have burned the village." He

124

looked anxiously across to where the swamps lay. "If our people are safe—"

"They won't be, until we destroy the Shining Stones," Trotting Fox said. "First we meet the enemy!"

Arvi crouched down to crawl with the rest as they came nearer and nearer. Cub Fox whispered, "The trader has slipped away by himself."

Arvi shook his head to indicate quiet. Like snakes the hunters crept along the shore. Then someone saw them and yelled in alarm—too late. The war party surged through the trees. Some turned to the beach with Trotting

Fox and sent flaming arrows into the raft of the Shining
Stones. Foxhead and the rest spread out through the forest.
From behind trees, they opened a furious assault with jave-
lins, spears, and arrows.

The Shining Stones were caught. From their raft,
clouds of black smoke arose. The enemy swam in all directions, but they were trapped between the hunters on the
beach and Hawk's warriors, who shot them from the high
lookouts.

Warth gathered the last of his men and fled south along
the beach. Arvi heard him shout a command and point to
the river. Foxhead's hunters burst from the forest.

"Warth escapes!" Foxhead shouted, and it seemed
possible, for Warth ran like a deer. Then from the trees
at the river bank a tall figure strode squarely into the chieftain's path.

"Quara!" Arvi cried. "Watch out—he throws an ax!"

Quara ducked. The ax spun over his shoulder. His
bowstring sang, and Warth stumbled forward to the
ground. The hunters caught up with the rest of the enemy,
and the fight was over.

126

The hunters yelled in triumph. They stamped on the ground and flung their weapons high, and the clamor was echoed from the lake village.

Signal fires were lit to summon the folk from the swamps, and dugout canoes sped to receive the hunters. And coming to the lake village for the first time, Trotting Fox walked straight to Hawk and offered his hand in allegiance.

"It was a mighty victory," he exulted. "Between us, we broke the Shining Stones as a nutshell is crushed between two stones!"

Hawk gripped the hunter's burly hand in his own. "It is a hopeful sign for the future," he exclaimed. "As we fought together, so we can work together, and our new village will stand year after year."

Soon all were together once more. The mountains echoed the thunder of drums, the chants of many voices, and the eerie music of the trader's flute.

There were stories of the victors: how Calling Hawk had defied the enemy, how Arvi had brought Trotting Fox and the hunters, and how Quara had slain Warth. It was said that the enemy chieftain had fallen to an arrow that held the magic of the Ancient Ones in its leaf-shaped stone.

The celebration went on, late into the night, for peace had come at last to the lake dwellers.